THE ANT AND THE GRASSHOPPER

Retold by BLAKE HOENA
Illustrations by LISK FENG
Music by DEAN JONES

CANTATA
LEARNING

WWW.CANTATALEARNING.COM

CANTATA
LEARNING

Published by Cantata Learning
1710 Roe Crest Drive
North Mankato, MN 56003
www.cantatalearning.com

Library of Congress Cataloging-in-Publication Data
Names: Hoena, B. A., author. | Feng, Lisk, illustrator. | Jones, Dean, 1966–
    composer. | Aesop.
Title: The ant and the grasshopper / retold by Blake Hoena ; illustrated by
    Lisk Feng ; music by Dean Jones.
Description: North Mankato, MN : Cantata Learning, [2018] | Series: Classic
    fables in rhythm and rhyme | Summary: A modern song retells the fable of
    the ant that works hard all summer long to feed her children and store
    food for the winter while her neighbor, a cheerful but lazy grasshopper,
    relaxes in the sun. Includes a brief introduction to Aesop, sheet music,
    glossary, discussion questions, and further reading.
Identifiers: LCCN 2017017553 (print) | LCCN 2017035539 (ebook) | ISBN
    9781684101474 (ebook) | ISBN 9781684101412 (hardcover : alk. paper) | ISBN
    9781684101849 (paperback : alk. paper)
Subjects: | CYAC: Behavior--Songs and music. | Fables. | Folklore. | Songs.
Classification: LCC PZ8.3.H667 (ebook) | LCC PZ8.3.H667 Ant 2018 (print) |
    DDC 398.2 [E] --dc23
LC record available at https://lccn.loc.gov/2017017553

978-1-68410-386-7 (hardcover)

Book design and art direction, Tim Palin Creative
Editorial direction, Kellie M. Hultgren
Music direction, Elizabeth Draper
Music arranged and produced by Dean Jones

Printed in the United States of America.
0398

ACCESS THE MUSIC!

SCAN
CODE
WITH
MOBILE
APP

CANTATALEARNING.COM

TIPS TO SUPPORT LITERACY AT HOME

WHY READING AND SINGING WITH YOUR CHILD IS SO IMPORTANT

Daily reading with your child leads to increased academic achievement. Music and songs, specifically rhyming songs, are a fun and easy way to build early literacy and language development. Music skills correlate significantly with both phonological awareness and reading development. Singing helps build vocabulary and speech development. And reading and appreciating music together is a wonderful way to strengthen your relationship.

READ AND SING EVERY DAY!

TIPS FOR USING CANTATA LEARNING BOOKS AND SONGS DURING YOUR DAILY STORY TIME

1. As you sing and read, point out the different words on the page that rhyme. Suggest other words that rhyme.

2. Memorize simple rhymes such as Itsy Bitsy Spider and sing them together. This encourages comprehension skills and early literacy skills.

3. Use the questions in the back of each book to guide your singing and storytelling.

4. Read the included sheet music with your child while you listen to the song. How do the music notes correlate to the words of the song?

5. Sing along on the go and at home. Access music by scanning the QR code on each Cantata book. You can also stream or download the music for free to your computer, smartphone, or mobile device.

Devoting time to daily reading shows that you are available for your child. Together, you are building language, literacy, and listening skills.

Have fun reading and singing!

Aesop was a storyteller who wrote hundreds of stories called **fables**. These short tales often had animals for characters. Each story is meant to teach a **moral**, or lesson.

In this fable, a grasshopper wants to play with an ant. But the ant is busy gathering food and **preparing** for winter. What lesson can be learned from the ant and the grasshopper?

Turn the page to find out. Remember to sing along!

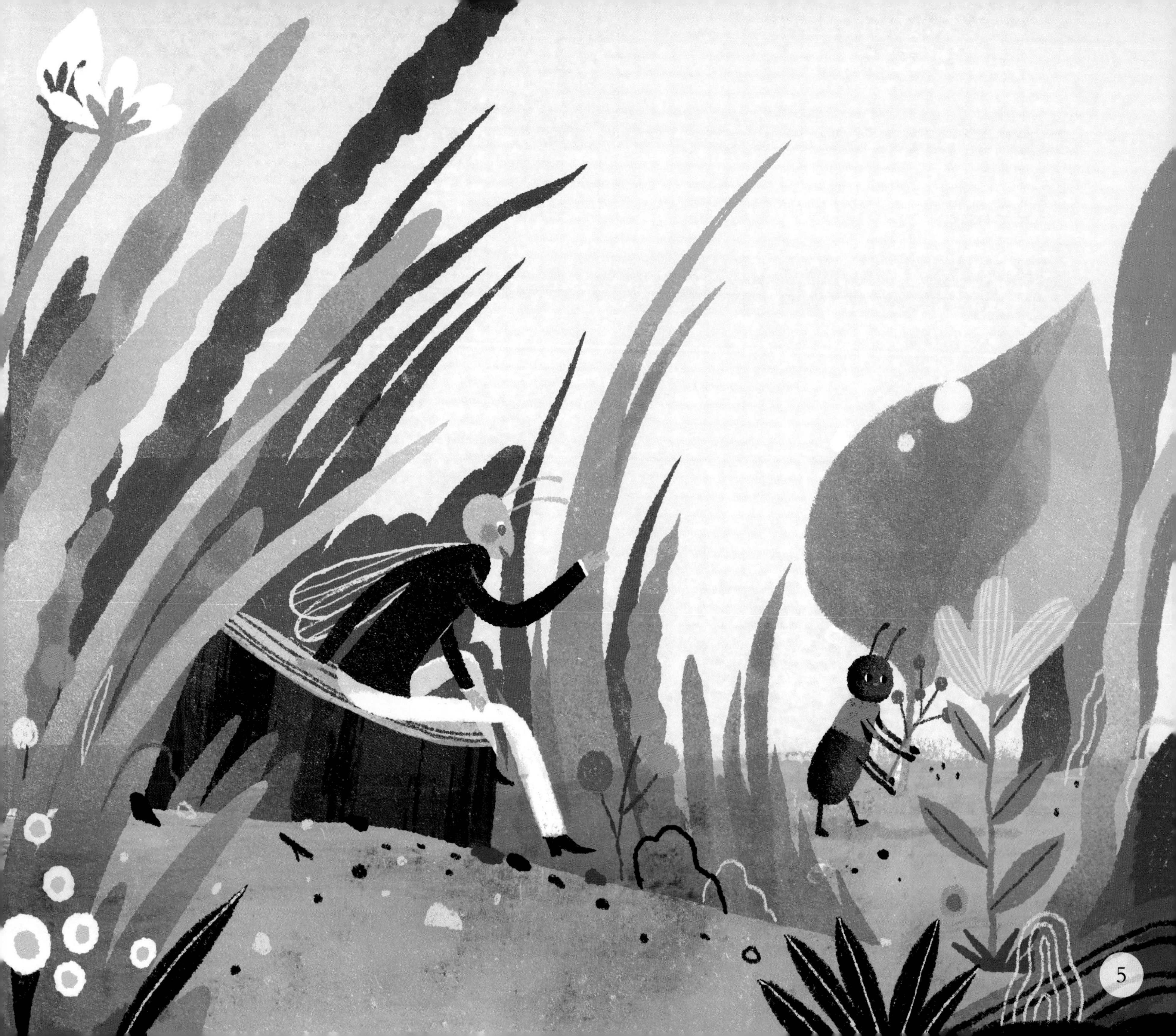

Hey, Ant, come play with me.
Hey, Ant, come play with me.
Hey, Ant, come play with me.

We'll have lots of fun, you'll see.

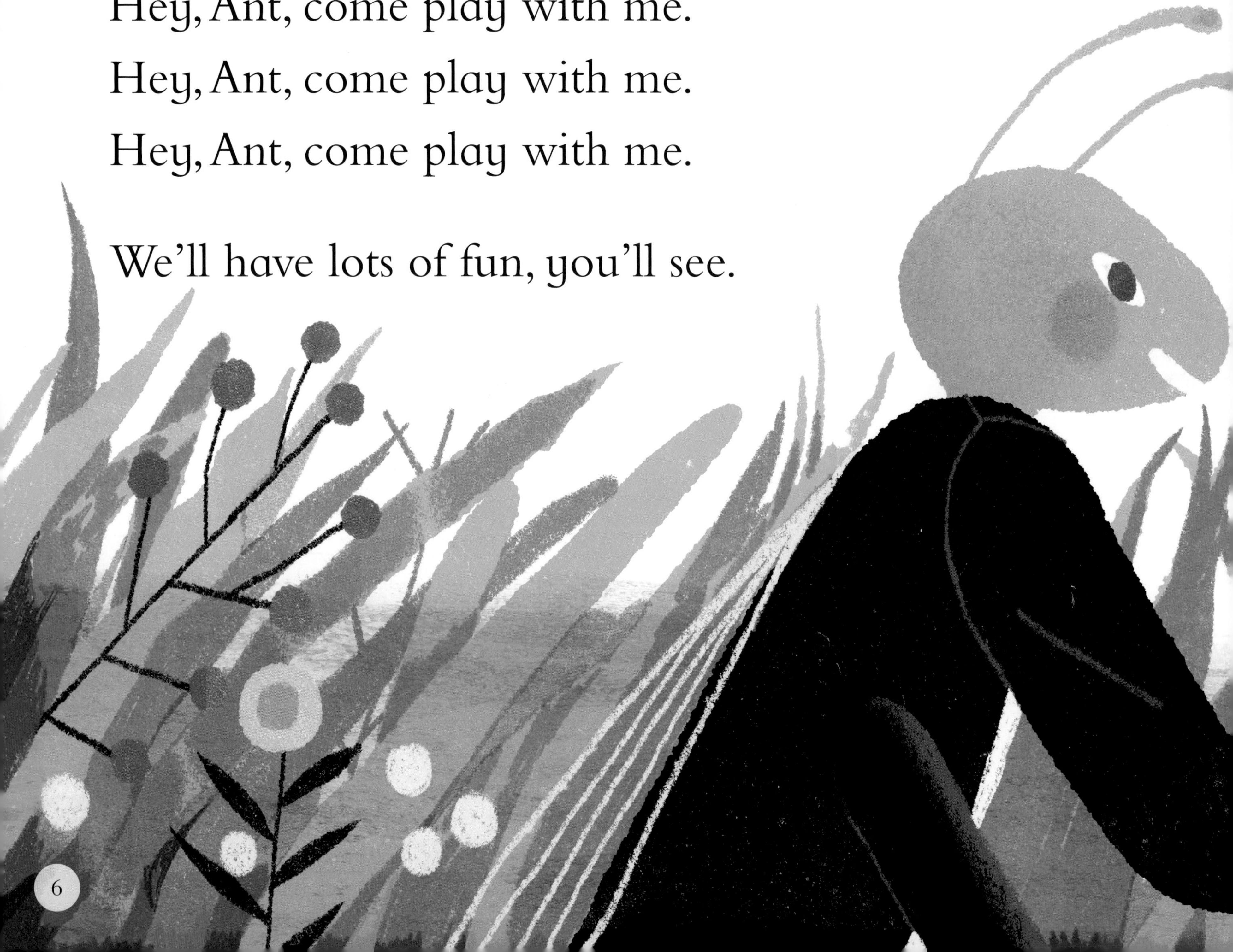

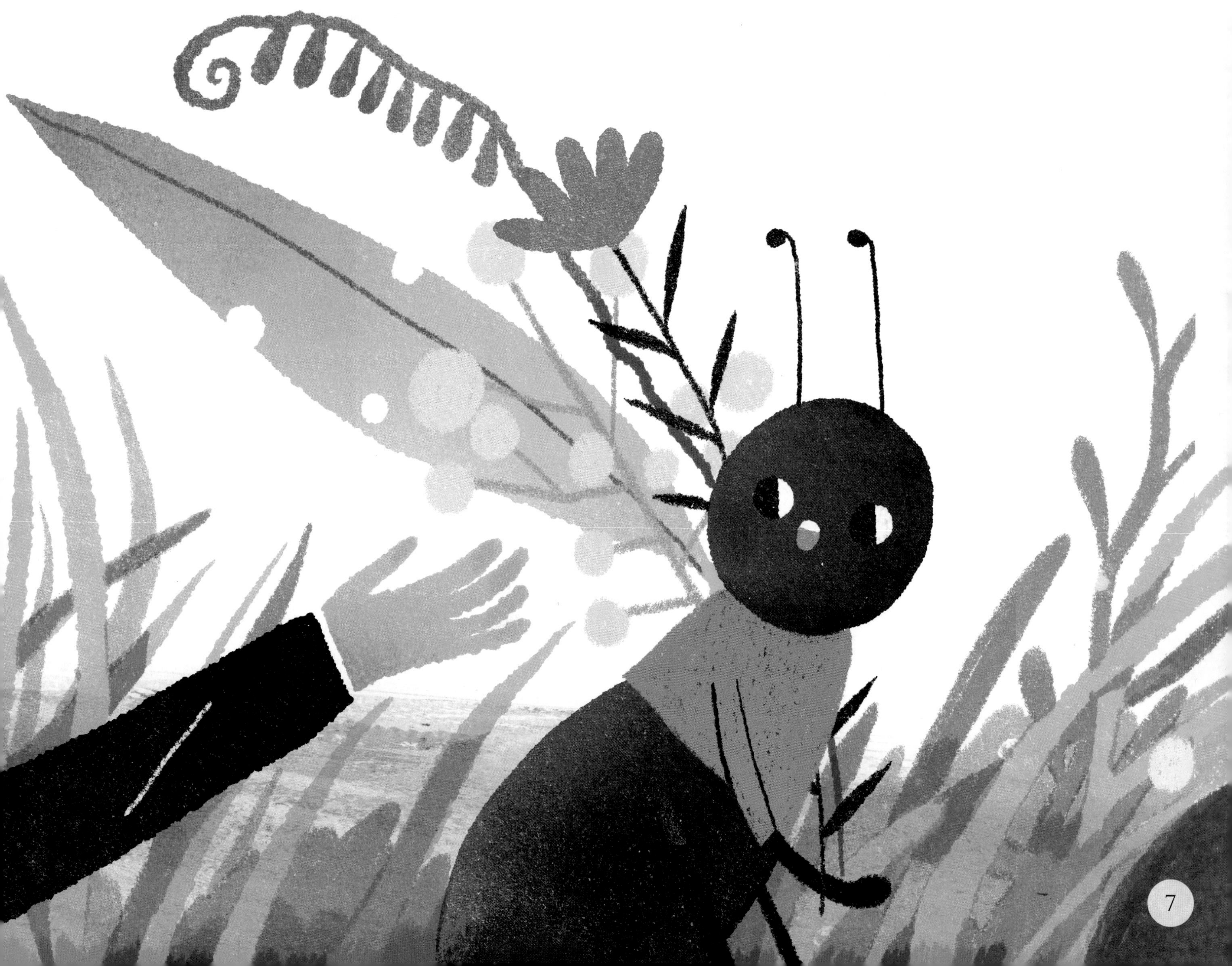

Not now. Not now. I need to gather food.
Not now. Not now. I need to gather food.

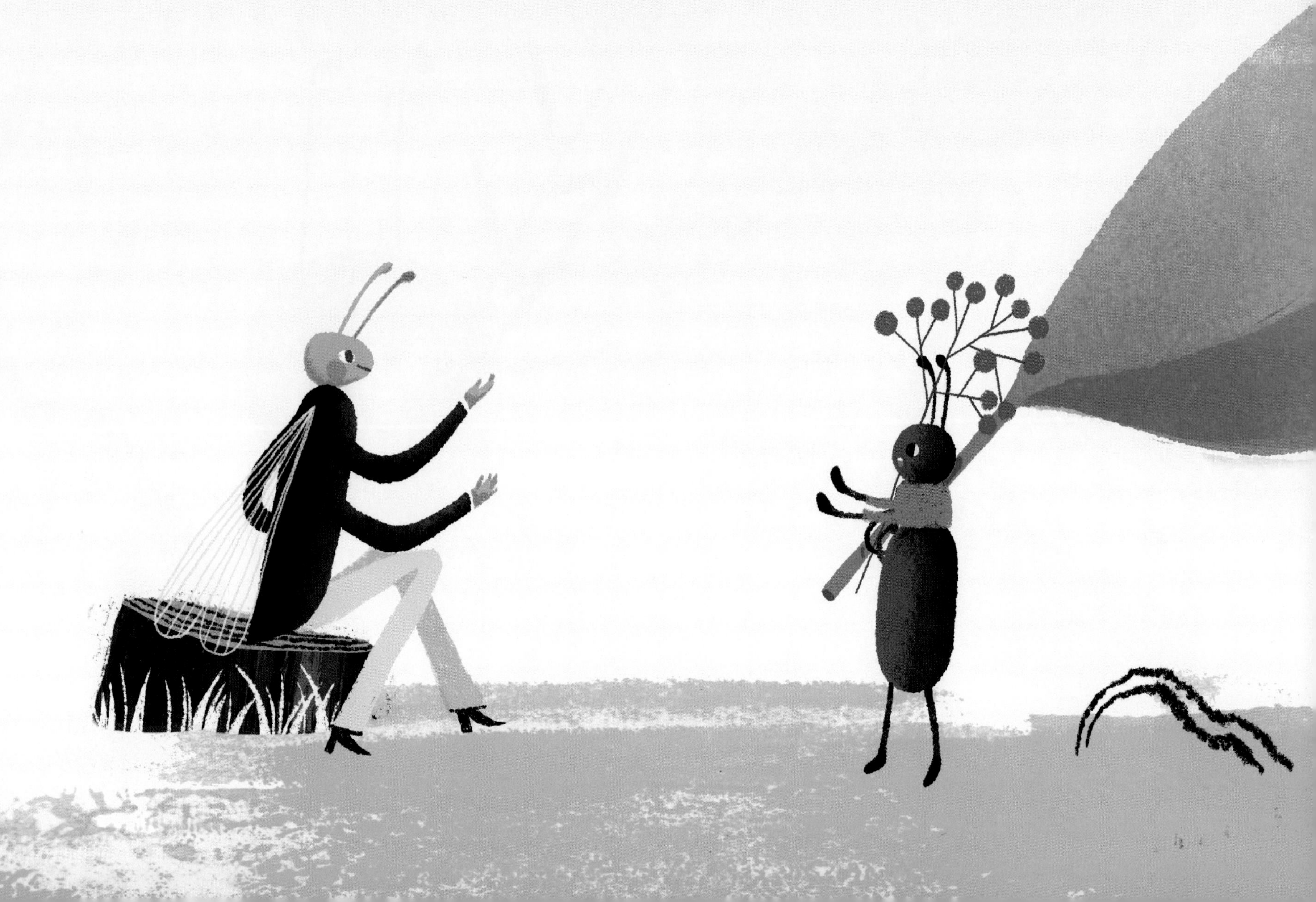

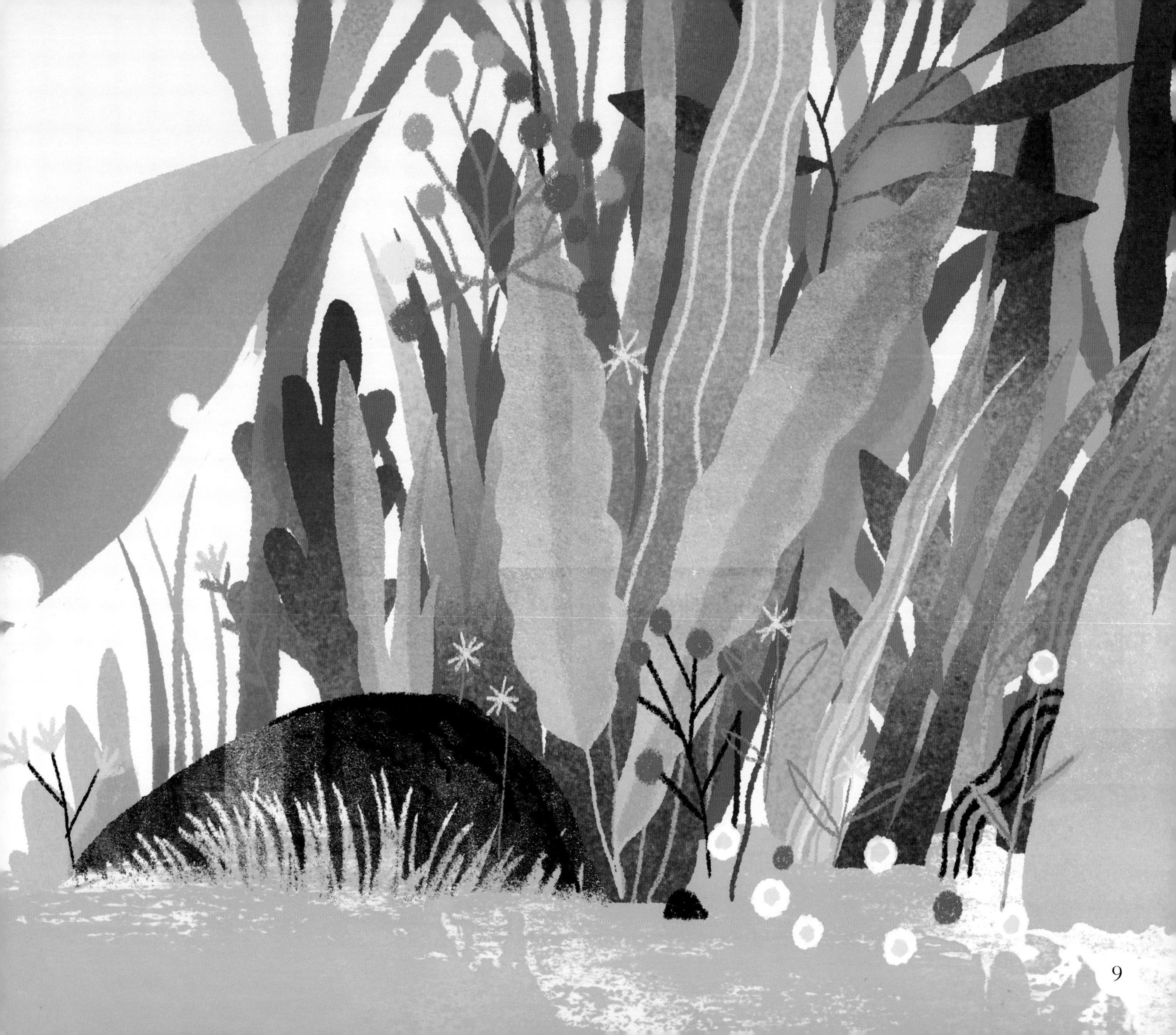

Oh, Ant, you work too much.
Oh, Ant, you work too much.
Oh, Ant, you work too much.

It's time for us to have some fun!

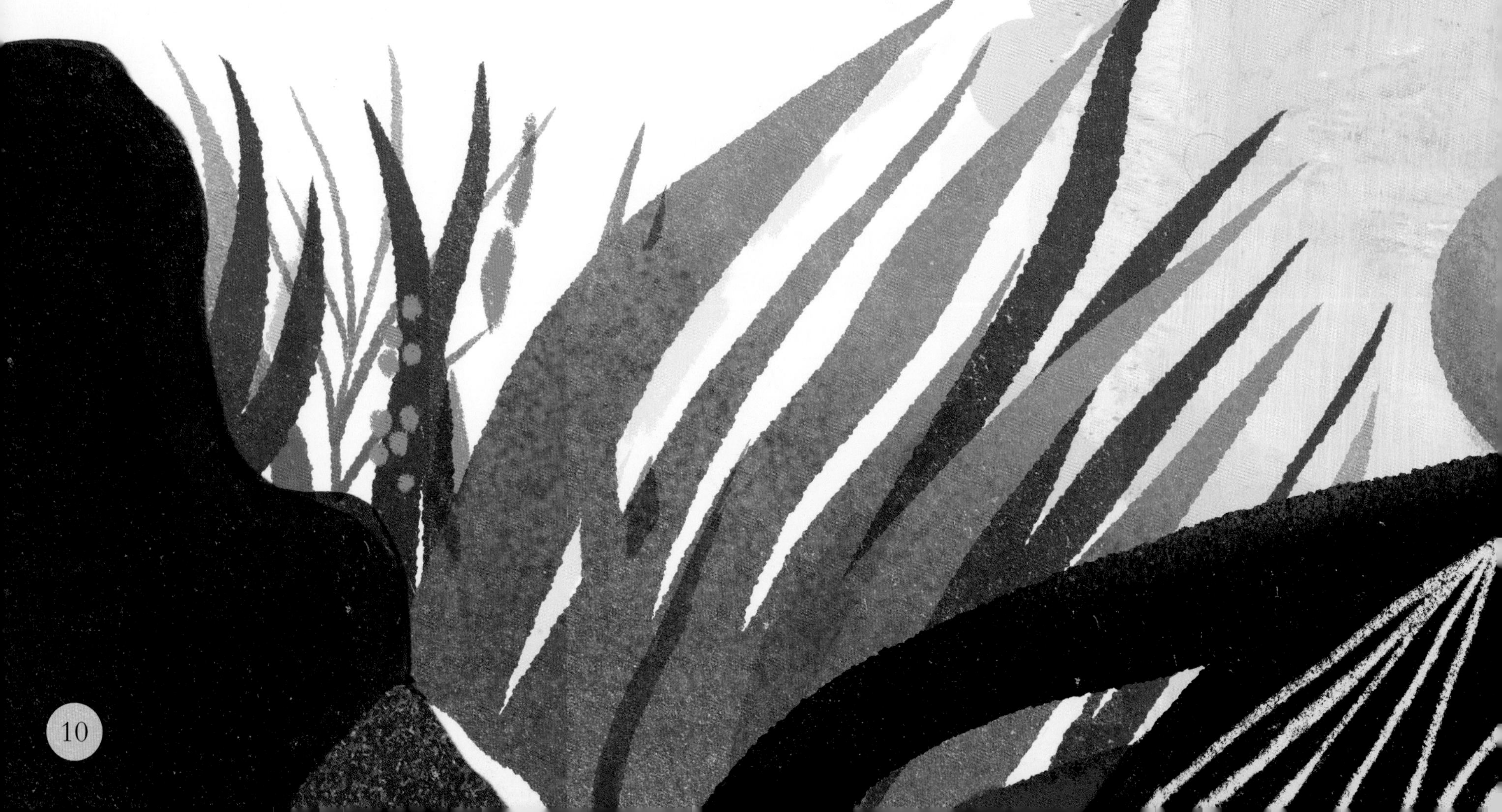

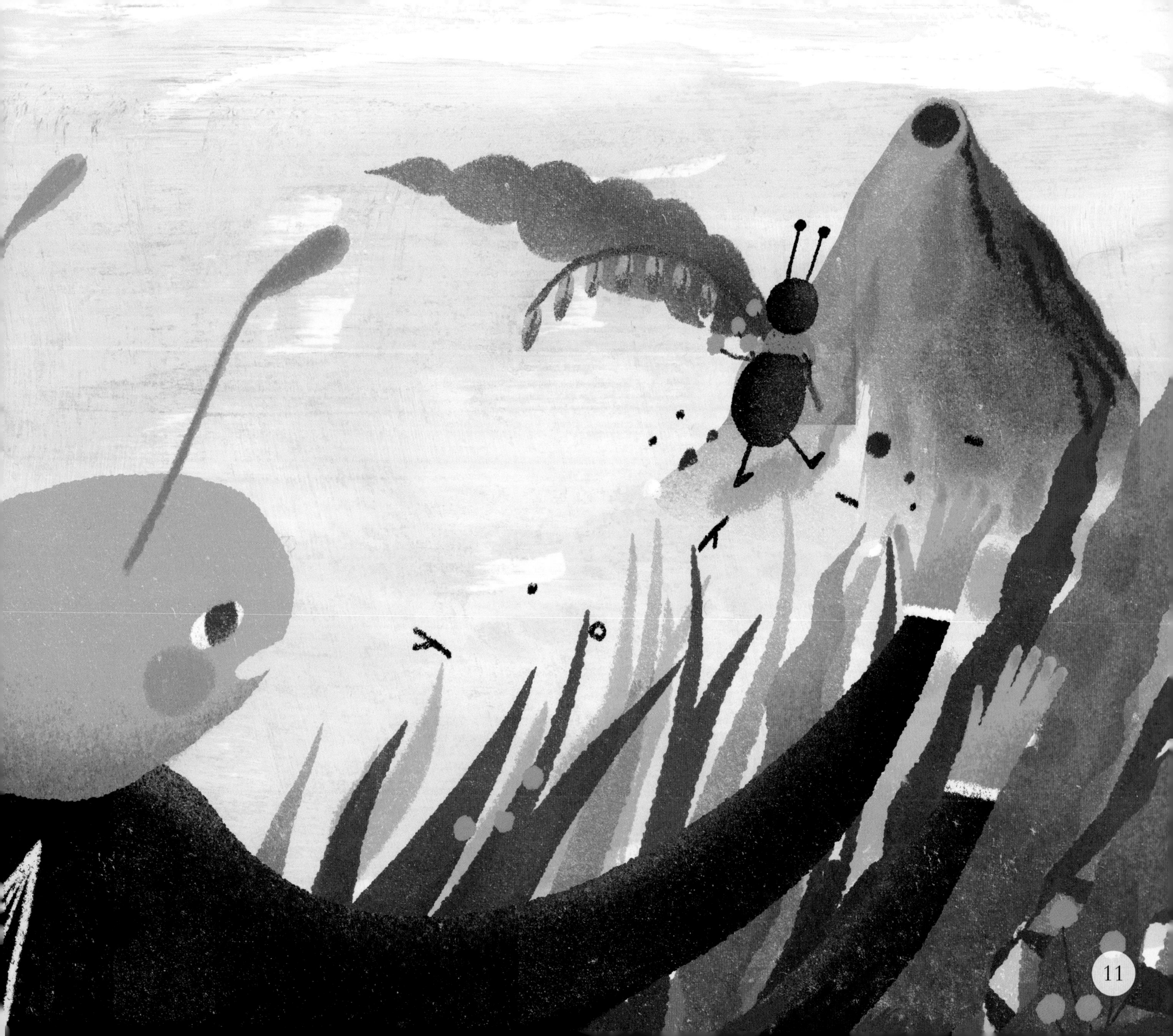

I can't. I can't. Winter's coming soon.
I can't. I can't. Winter's coming soon.

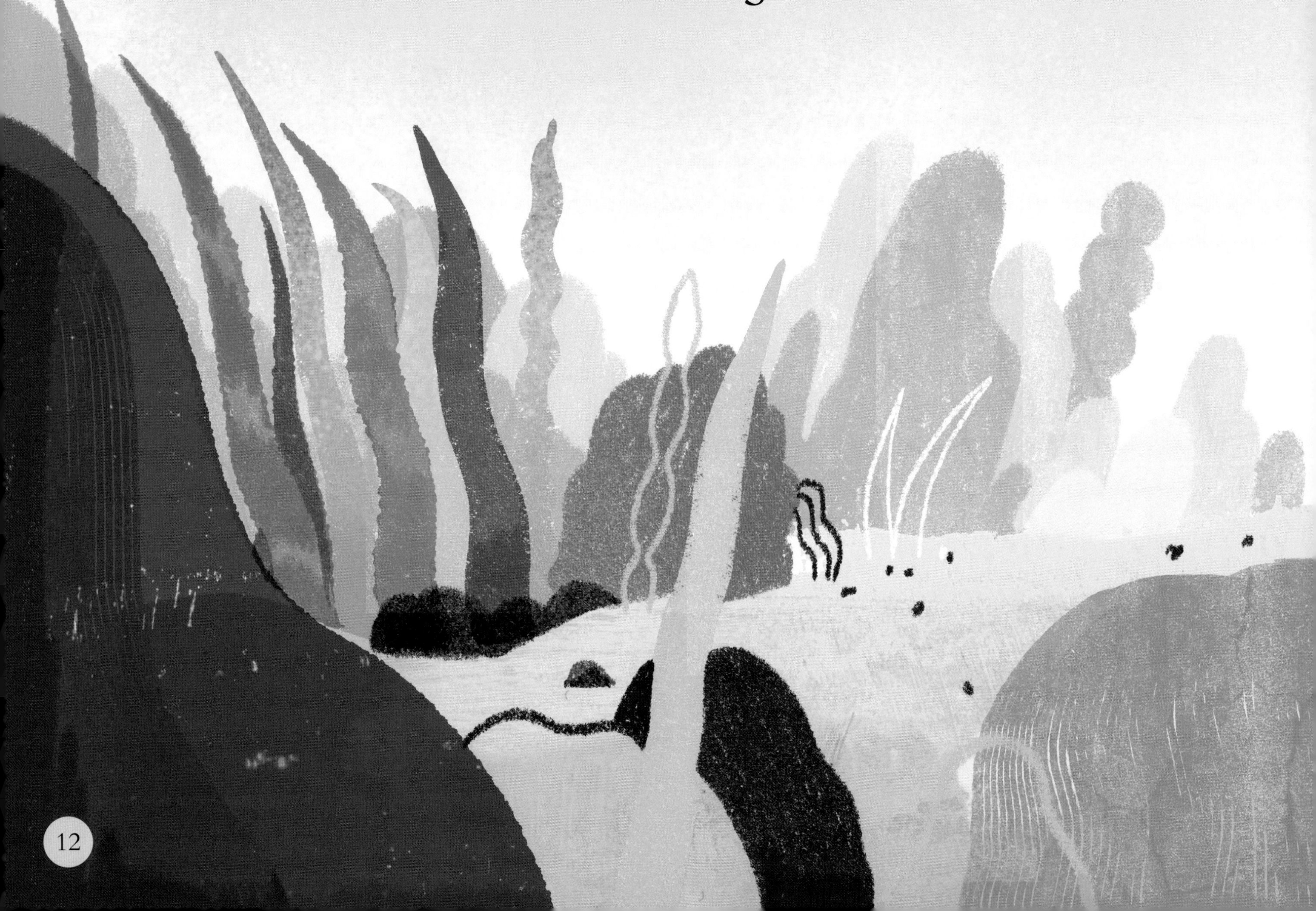

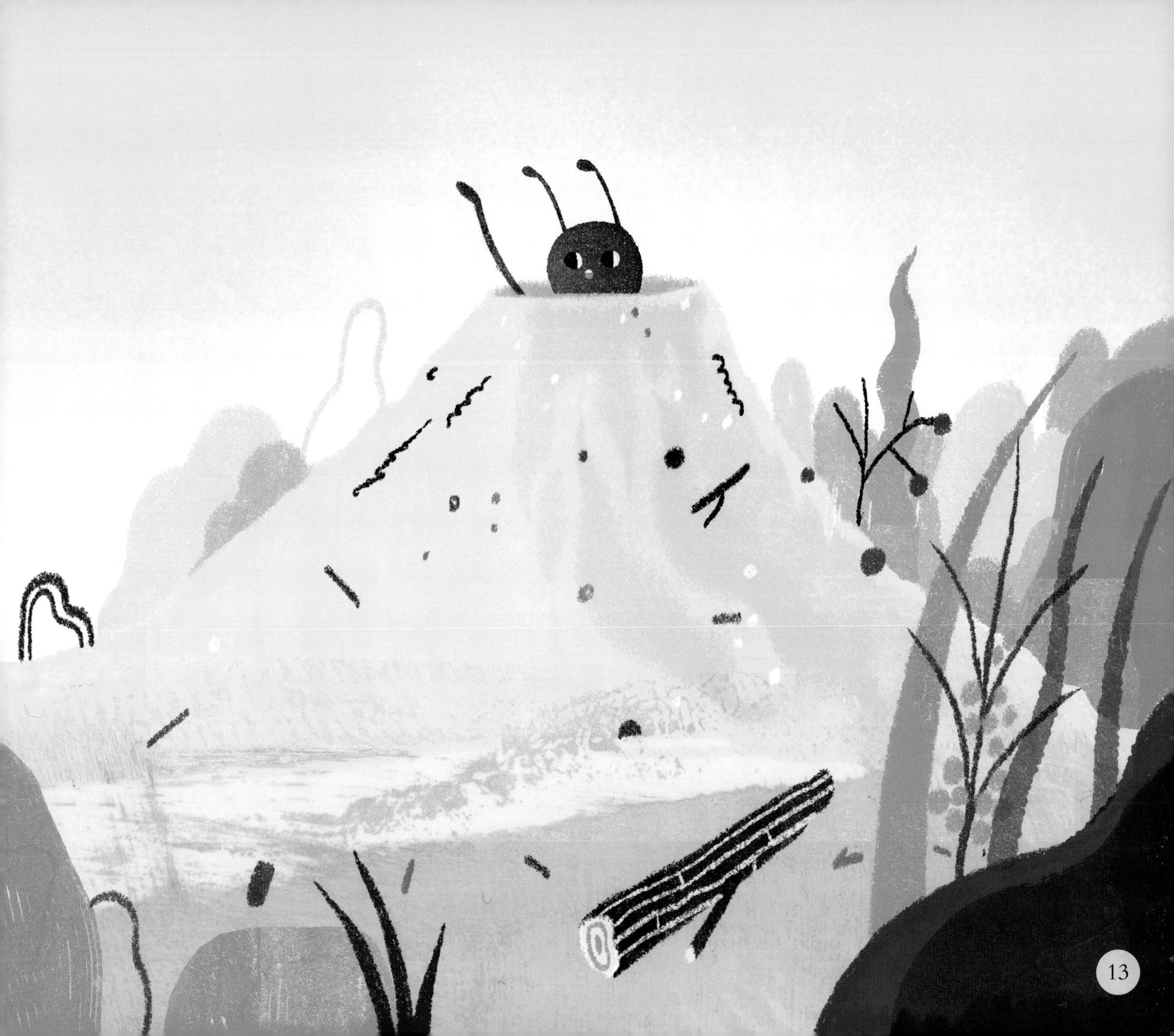

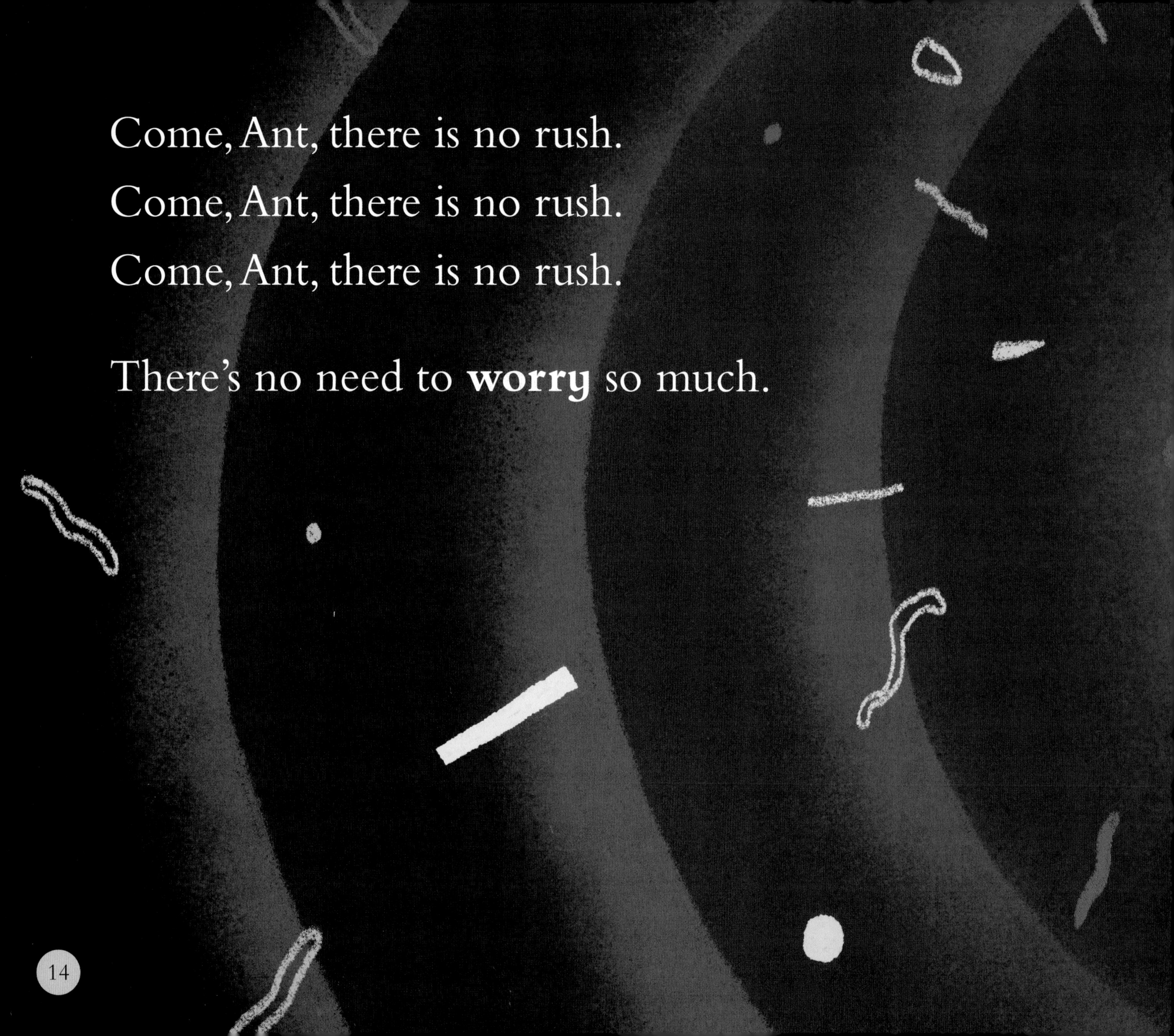

Come, Ant, there is no rush.
Come, Ant, there is no rush.
Come, Ant, there is no rush.

There's no need to **worry** so much.

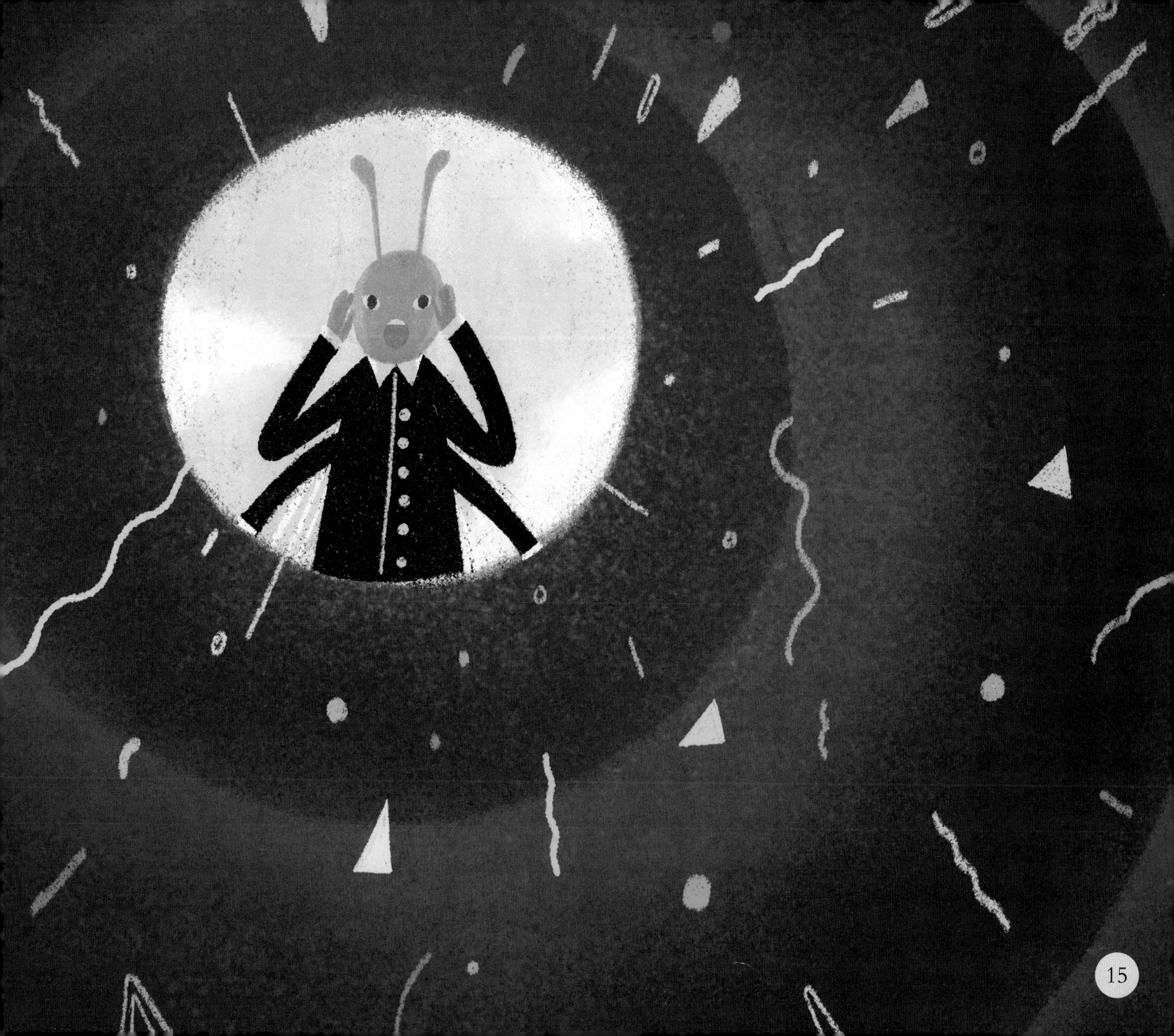

You should, you should start preparing too.
You should, you should start preparing too.

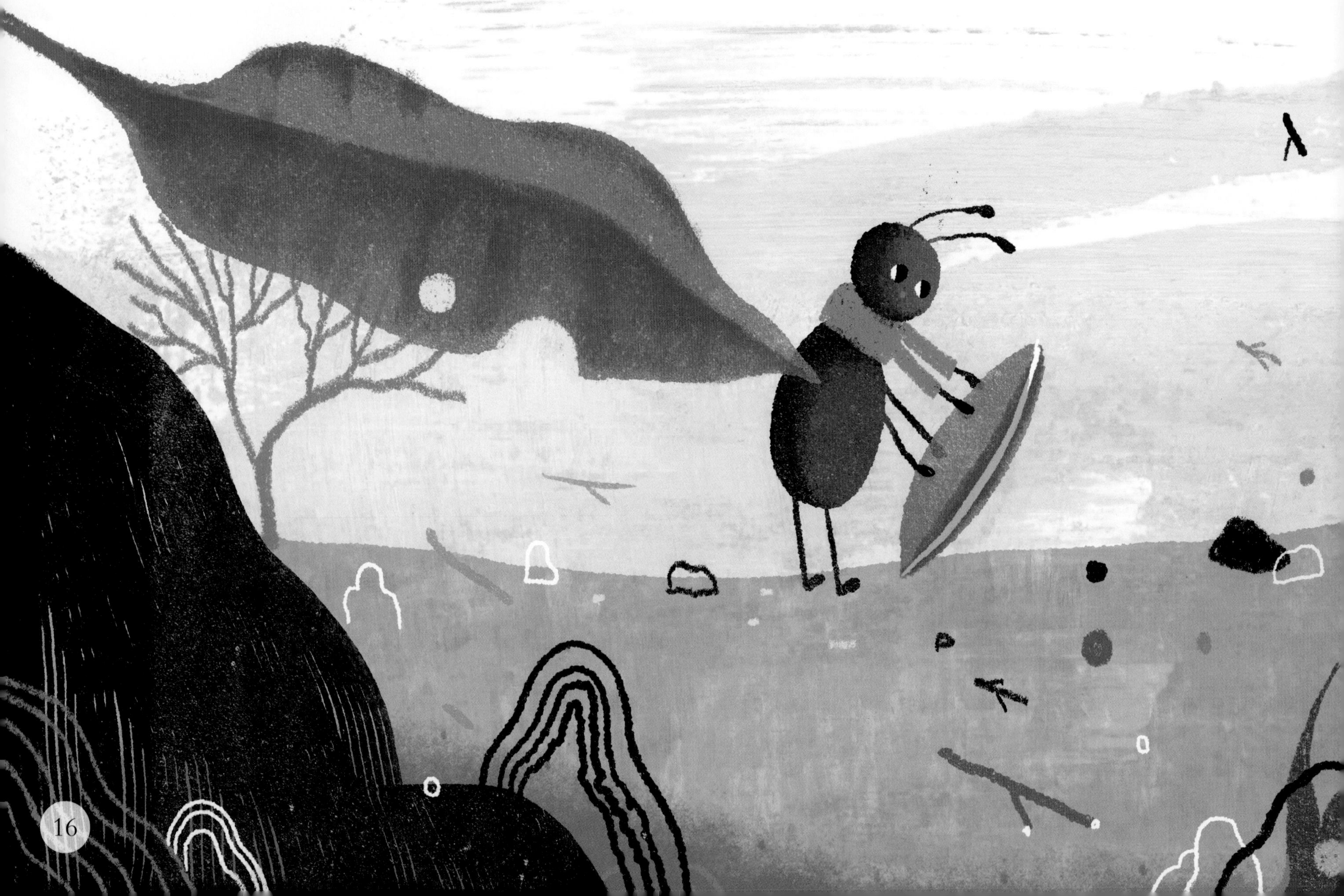

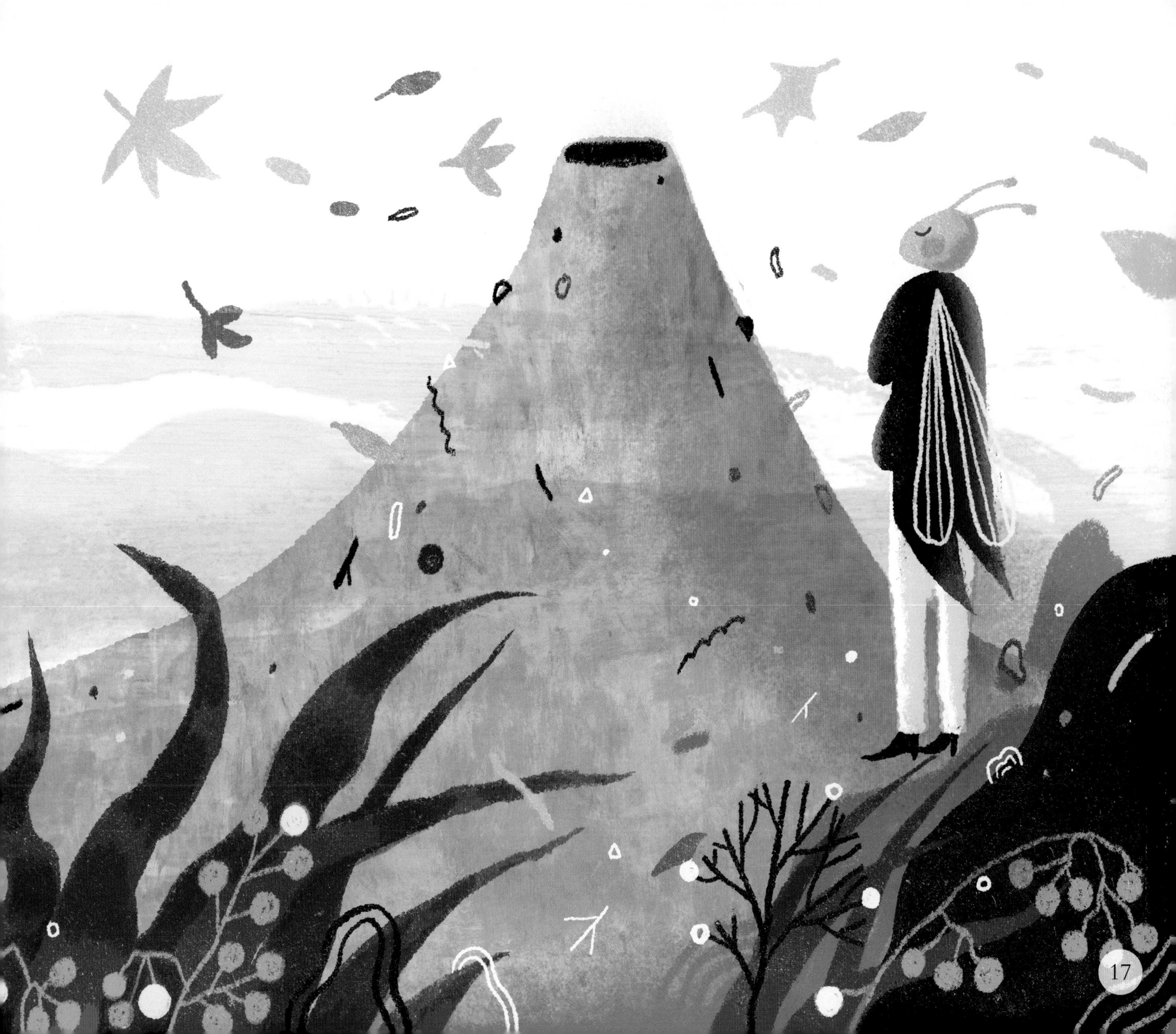

Brrr, Ant, what will I do?

Brrr, Ant, what will I do?

Brrr, Ant, what will I do?

Winter's here and I have no food!

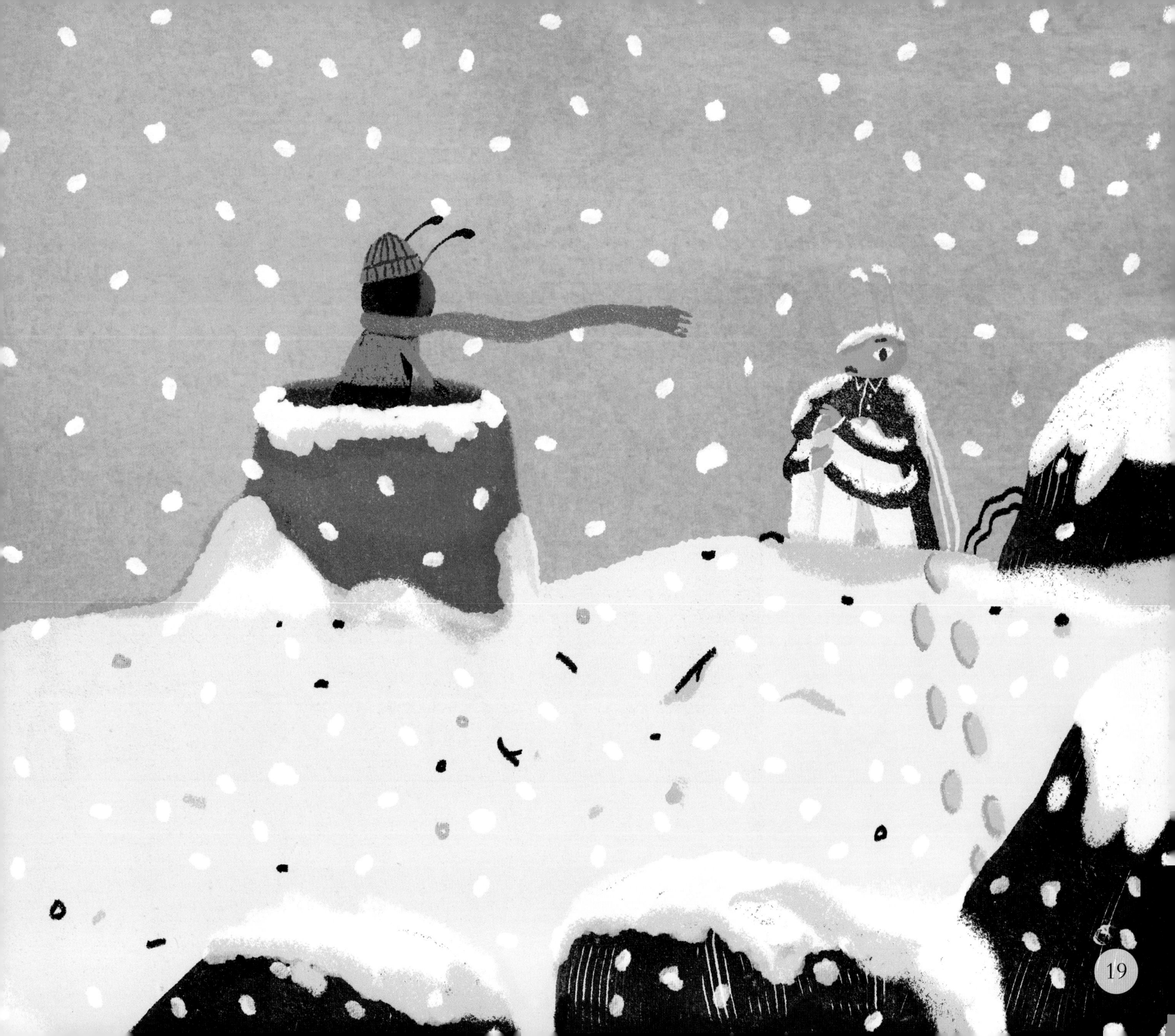

Come in, come in, for I have plenty to eat.
Come in, come in, for I have plenty to eat.

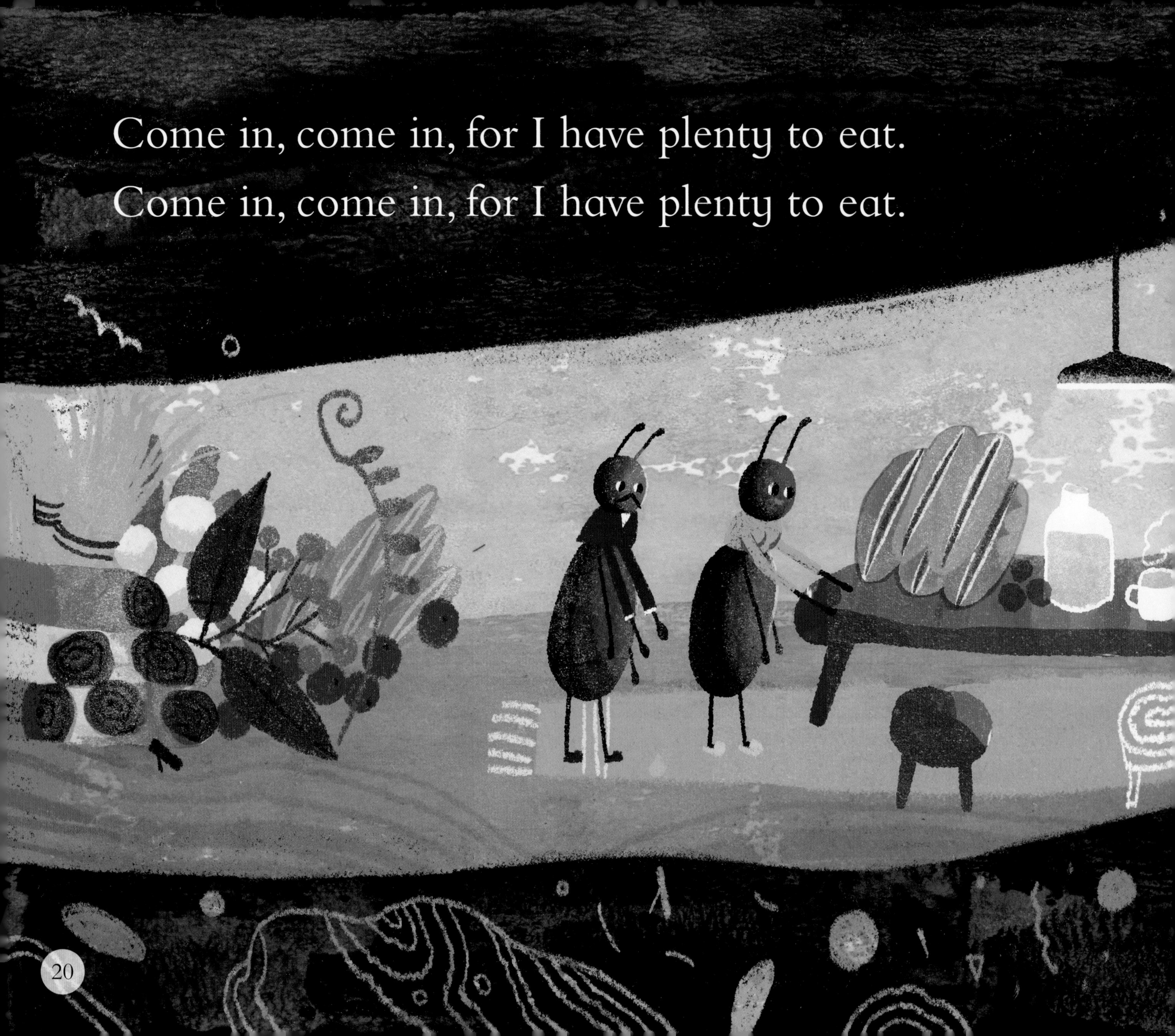

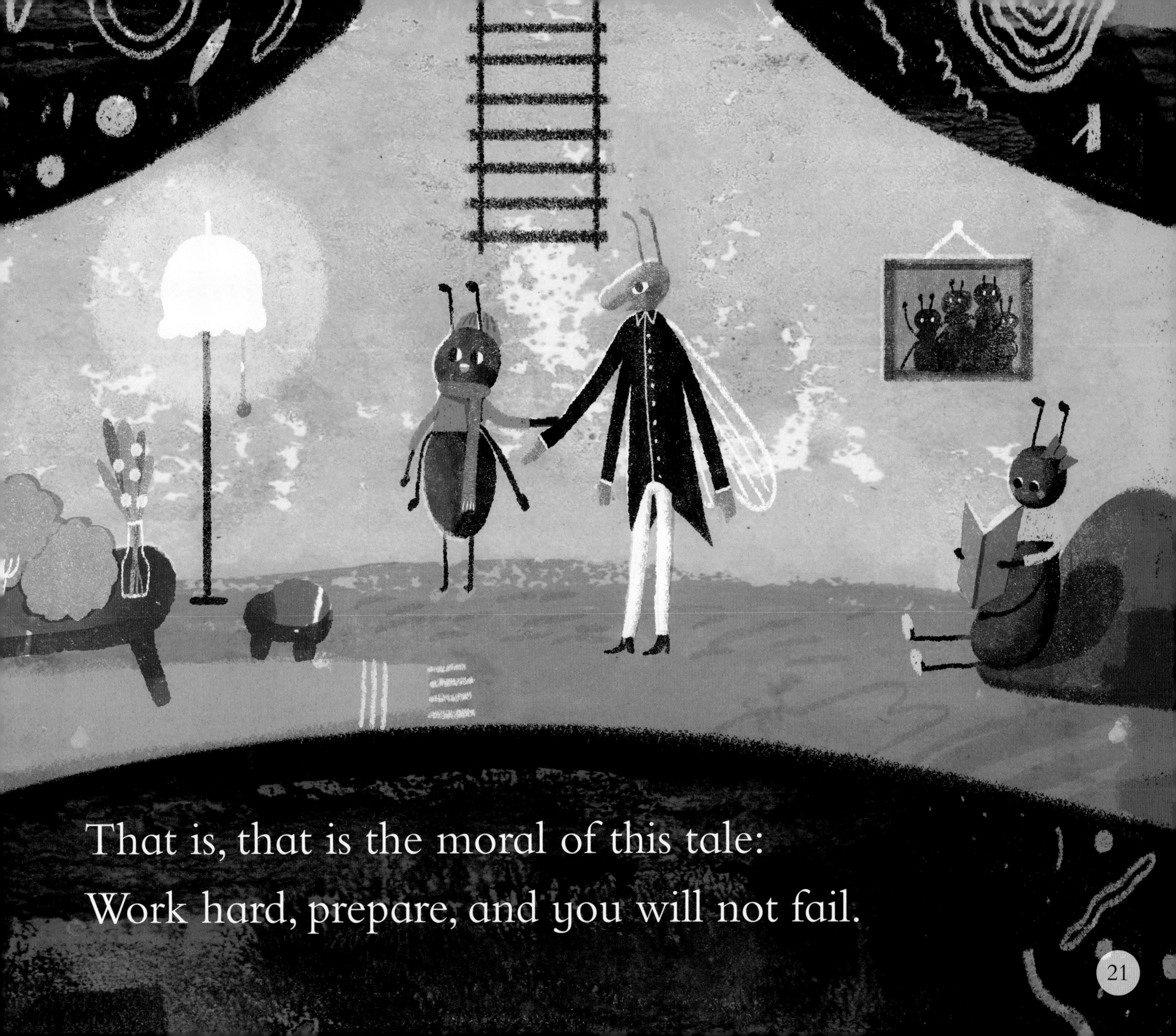

That is, that is the moral of this tale:
Work hard, prepare, and you will not fail.

SONG LYRICS
The Ant and the Grasshopper

Hey, Ant, come play with me.
Hey, Ant, come play with me.
Hey, Ant, come play with me.
We'll have lots of fun, you'll see.

Not now. Not now. I need to gather food.
Not now. Not now. I need to gather food.

Oh, Ant, you work too much.
Oh, Ant, you work too much.
Oh, Ant, you work too much.
It's time for us to have some fun!

I can't. I can't. Winter's coming soon.
I can't. I can't. Winter's coming soon.

Come, Ant, there is no rush.
Come, Ant, there is no rush.
Come, Ant, there is no rush.
There's no need to worry so much.

You should, you should start preparing too.
You should, you should start preparing too.

Brrr, Ant, what will I do?
Brrr, Ant, what will I do?
Brrr, Ant, what will I do?
Winter's here and I have no food!

Come in, come in, for I have plenty to eat.
Come in, come in, for I have plenty to eat.

[Sung together]
That is, that is the moral of this tale:
Work hard, prepare, and you will not fail.

The Ant and the Grasshopper

Jazz/Dance Hall
Dean Jones

Verse

G D G D G D G
1. Hey, Ant, come play with me. Hey, Ant, come play with me. Hey, Ant, come play with me. We'll have lots of fun, you'll see.

Chorus

G D G
Not now. Not now. I need to gath - er food. Not now. Not now. I need to gath - er food.

Verse 2
Oh, Ant, you work too much.
Oh, Ant, you work too much.
Oh, Ant, you work too much.
It's time for us to have some fun!

Chorus
I can't. I can't. Winter's coming soon.
I can't. I can't. Winter's coming soon.

Verse 3
Come, Ant, there is no rush.
Come, Ant, there is no rush.
Come, Ant, there is no rush.
There's no need to worry so much.

Chorus
You should, you should start preparing too.
You should, you should start preparing too.

Verse 4
Brrr, Ant, what will I do?
Brrr, Ant, what will I do?
Brrr, Ant, what will I do?
Winter's here and I have no food!

Chorus
Come in, come in, for I have plenty to eat.
Come in, come in, for I have plenty to eat.

Interlude

G D G

Outro

G D G D G D G
That is, that is the mor - al of this tale: Work hard, pre-pare, and you will not fail.

ACCESS THE MUSIC!
SCAN CODE WITH MOBILE APP
CANTATALEARNING.COM

GLOSSARY

Aesop—a legendary storyteller who is said to have lived in ancient Greece around 600 BCE

fables—short stories that often have animal characters and teach a lesson

moral—a lesson, often found in a fable or story

preparing—getting ready for something

worry—to be upset or feel concerned

GUIDED READING ACTIVITIES

1. The ant prepares for winter, while the grasshopper plays around. Is one choice better than the other, or can you do both? Why, or why not? Are you more like the ant or the grasshopper?

2. Listen to this song with a friend. Then sing it yourselves, with one of you singing the ant's parts and the other singing the grasshopper's parts. This is called singing a duet.

3. The ant is preparing for winter. What things do you do to prepare for winter? Draw a picture of your favorite part of preparing for winter.

TO LEARN MORE

Hardyman, Robyn. *What Is a Fable?* New York: Britannica Educational, 2014.

Hoena, Blake. *The Lion and the Mouse.* North Mankato, MN: Cantata Learning, 2018.

Hoena, Blake. *Shoo, Fly, Don't Bother Me.* North Mankato, MN: Cantata Learning, 2016.

White, Mark. *The Ant and the Grasshopper: A Retelling of Aesop's Fable.* Mankato, MN: Picture Window, 2012.